Dear Molly, Dear Olive

Olive Becomes Famous
(and Hopes She Can Become Un-Famous)

written by
Megan Atwood

illustrated by
Gareth Llewhellin
and Lucy Fleming

PICTURE WINDOW BOOKS
a capstone imprint

Picture Window Books are published by Capstone
1710 Roe Crest Drive
North Mankato, Minnesota 56003
www.mycapstone.com

Library of Congress Cataloging-in-Publication Data
Names: Atwood, Megan, author. | Llewhellin, Gareth, illustrator. | Fleming, Lucy, illustrator.
Title: Olive becomes famous (and hopes she can become un-famous) /
by Megan Atwood ; illustrated by Gareth Llewhellin, Lucy Fleming.
Description: North Mankato, Minnesota : Picture Window Books, [2018] |
Series: Dear Molly, Dear Olive | Summary: Ten-year old Olive is going to
be in a commercial, but she really is not sure she can land the gymnastics
stunt written for it, and her cross-country email pal Molly is jealous and
determined to get into a commercial herself (pretty much any commerical
will do)—and now their friendship is threatened by their increasingly testy emails.
Identifiers: LCCN 2018009426 (print) | LCCN 2018009718 (ebook) |
ISBN 9781515829249 (eBook PDF) | ISBN 9781515829225 (library binding) |
ISBN 9781684360413 (paperback)
Subjects: LCSH: Best friends—Juvenile fiction. | Pen pals—Juvenile fiction. |
Television commercials—Juvenile fiction. | Electronic mail messages—Juvenile fiction. |
Friendship—Juvenile fiction. | Envy—Juvenile fiction. | CYAC: Best friends—Fiction. |
Friendship--Fiction. | Pen pals—Fiction. | Television advertising—Fiction. |
Jealousy—Fiction.
Classification: LCC PZ7.A8952 (ebook) | LCC PZ7.A8952 Oj 2018 (print) |
DDC 813.6 [Fic] —dc23
LC record available at https://lccn.loc.gov/2018009426

Editor: Gina Kammer
Designers: Aruna Rangarajan and Tracy McCabe
Production Specialist: Kris Wilfahrt

Design Elements: Shutterstock

Printed in Canada.
PA020

Table of Contents

Dear Molly,
Dear Olive

Molly and Olive are best friends — best friends who've never met! Two years ago, in second grade, they signed up for a cross-country Pen Pal Club. Their friendship was instant.

Molly and Olive send each other letters and email. They send postcards, notes, and little gifts too. Molly lives in New York City with her mom and younger brother. Olive lives on a farm near Sergeant Bluff, Iowa, with her parents. The girls' lives are very different from one another. But Molly and Olive understand each other better than anyone.

6

Chapter 1

Olive Sees Stars

Olive

Walking through a farm supply store isn't the most exciting thing to do on a Saturday. But NEXT Saturday gymnastics would start.

"Next weekend, we'll go into the city so you can practice with Coach, my mom said. I couldn't wait. She nodded toward a bag of cattle feed, and I helped her lift it onto the cart.

"This year I WILL do a full. Maybe I'll even do a DOUBLE full," I said.

Mom smiled. "I can't wait to see you do a twist, my dear. But a double twist? Save something for when you're in fifth grade."

"It's called a full or a double full, Mom." I put my hands on my hips and pretended to be mad. She copied me and gave me a mock mad look back. We both giggled.

The full was something I couldn't seem to get down right. I'd been complaining about it to Molly for weeks. This upcoming season of gymnastics, I WOULD get the full down. That gave me four whole months to practice.

"Did I hear you say you do gymnastics?" a man boomed.

"Oh, yes. Our Olive here is a regular Gabby Douglas," said Mom.

The man held out his hand. "I'm Matt Miller, the Mattress Guy. Maybe you saw me on TV?"

I looked at him closely. I did recognize him! He had been in these crazy commercials with lots of sound effects and big letters.

My mom said, "Oh, yeah! You have that mattress store in downtown Sioux City, right? I've seen your commercials." She took a big breath and said in a commercial voice, "'You'll sleep like a baby on a —"

"Miller mattress!" the man interrupted. He laughed and put his hand on his belly. I decided right then and there that I liked him.

"I am having a 'Spring into Savings Sale,'" he said, looking at me. "And I think a talented gymnast like yourself is exactly who we need! What do you think about being the star of my next commercial?"

9

My heart beat a million miles a minute. Me? In a commercial! I nodded and bounced a little. "Can I, Mom?" I asked.

She squeezed my shoulder and said, "Let me grab your dad, and we can talk about the whole thing as a family. I'll be right back."

She left me standing with Mr. Miller, and I felt really shy. He said, "Sorry to bother you. I just heard you could do a twist. So I'd just want you to do two back handsprings and a twist — you can do that, right?"

I almost said, "It's called a full!" but stopped myself, because then it suddenly felt real. A COMMERCIAL. ON TV.

I should have been honest right then. I should have told him the truth. But I couldn't seem to open my mouth. So I did something kind of dumb: I nodded.

"Great!" he boomed. "Don't worry — you don't have to say anything in the commercial." He smiled at me and patted my back.

My mom came back with my dad, and they both said at the same time, "Yes!" Then my mom said, "If Olive wants to do it, then we're okay with it."

Mr. Miller winked at me. "Yep, I think she wants to. We already have the moves down."

While the adults exchanged information, my head swam. How was I supposed to do a full? I wished I could talk to Molly.

The whole way back to the farm, I thought about what I would write her. When we got to

our house, I sprinted to the computer.

Dear Molly,

You are never going to guess what happened to me today! I'm going to be in a commercial!

The excitement of it came rushing back. People would see me on TV! So cool! But Molly had just enrolled in an acting class, so she probably knew all sorts of famous people already. Plus, she lived in New York, where tons of commercials were made each day. Thinking about that made me feel just a little silly. I decided against telling her how worried I was. She might think I was just a hick who didn't know anything about acting. I finished the letter.

It's so cool — I get to use my gymnastics. I'll do two back handsprings and then a full. (That means a whole twist in the air.) I am pretty sure everyone will see the commercial. Maybe I could even be in more commercials if this one works out!

I can't wait to hear how your acting class is going. Just think: BOTH of us as actors.

Best friends forever,

Olive

I sent the email and closed down the computer. I felt pretty good about everything that day. Even if I'd just agreed to do something I couldn't do.

Maybe I didn't feel that great after all.

14

Chapter 2

Molly's Method and Madness

Molly

Sabrina kept talking about method acting, so I had to pretend I knew what she meant. She'd been in SEVEN commercials already, and she was just 10 years old like me! She was also really pretty — she had long black hair and olive-brown skin that glowed.

She sat by ME in my new acting class. So. That was pretty cool.

She'd never be Olive. But if I had to be friends with someone who lived close to me, Sabrina was the obvious choice.

It was only the first class we'd had, but already I loved it. We did all sorts of things, including improvisation scenes where we had to make things up as we went along. I was the best at that. Then we practiced speaking from our bellies so people could hear us. But really, the most exciting thing to me was meeting Sabrina.

After class, she and I waited on the sidewalk for our parents to come. Her dad was picking her up in a car. My mom and I would walk home together — the class was in a college building that wasn't too far away from our apartment.

"You've really been in seven commercials?" I asked Sabrina.

Sabrina, who was lots taller than me, looked down, but not really in my eyes. "Yep," she said, "and I think I have a couple more coming up."

I wanted to be in a commercial so badly. I felt dumb that I hadn't already. But I thought about Olive and how she never thought I was dumb, so I got a little braver. "Um, how do you get in commercials? Do you think I could get in one?"

Sabrina stared at me for a long time. I thought maybe she forgot I'd asked a question. I was going to poke her, but then she said, "You were pretty good at class today. I bet you could be in a commercial. I could even see if the next one could have us both try out."

I froze. TRYOUTS? FOR A COMMERCIAL?

I thought I might explode with happiness. "That might be cool," my voice squeaked.

Just as I was about to say something else, a car pulled up in front of us. "Here's my dad! See you next week," Sabrina said, throwing her long dark hair over her shoulder. "I bet we could have a lot of fun," she said as she got in and closed the door. The car pulled away.

Someone put a hand on my shoulder, and I jumped. It was just my mom.

"Well, goodness, you were thinking hard on something," she said.

I turned to her excitedly. "That was Sabrina!" I said. "She's been in, like, ten commercials!" I knew Sabrina said seven, but I liked to round up in these stories.

"That's impressive," Mom said, her eyebrows shooting up. "I wonder why she's taking a beginner acting class. . . ."

I had no time for silly questions like that. "It doesn't matter. What DOES matter is she said we might be able to BOTH try out for a new commercial! ISN'T THAT COOL?" I couldn't help it — my voice got louder and louder. Mom called it my "bullhorn voice."

"Molly," she said, "I hear you! Lower your voice a little, honey. That is indeed pretty cool. Do you know when this tryout might happen?"

We'd reached our apartment, and our doorman, Jared, nodded at us. "Evening, ladies," he said, and tipped his red hat. He opened the door for us.

"Hi, Jared!" I said, slipping inside. "I don't know when. But it will definitely happen!" I said happily as we reached our elevator.

"Hmm," Mom said. "Well, that's great, sweetie." But the way she said it made it sound like she didn't think it was that great.

Never tell a mom something you should tell your best friend. Moms just couldn't be as excited for you. It was like a law of nature.

Inside our apartment, I sprinted across the wood floor, ran down the hallway to my room, and hopped on the computer.

I hit the "compose" button before I even checked my email. I started writing fast.

Dear Olive,

YOU WILL NEVER GUESS WHAT!

But then I saw that Olive had already written, so I clicked on her email.

And my heart sunk all the way to my toes.

I couldn't believe it. OLIVE was going to be in a commercial. Not even just a tryout — a real commercial. My eyes got all fuzzy, and my stomach turned like a flipped pancake.

I got up and paced around my room.

WAS EVERYONE IN A COMMERCIAL BUT ME?

I decided that I couldn't really compare to what Olive had going on. But Sabrina could. So I sat down and wrote a long email about my new friend, Sabrina — the most talented actor I knew. I hit send and then threw myself on the bed. If acting was so great, why was I crying?

Olive Twists Her Story Around

I re-read Molly's email to me:

Dear Olive,

YOU WILL NEVER GUESS WHAT! I met the COOLEST girl in my acting class. Her name is Sabrina, and she's been in TEN commercials, and I'm pretty sure we're going to be in one together soon too. She knows more about acting than anyone else I know. Isn't this good timing? You get to be in a commercial, and I meet another friend who's been in TEN TIMES more commercials than you? It's like all my best friends are famous now.

Okay, gotta go. I need to practice my acting for the audition that's probably coming up.

XOXOXO,

Molly

"All my best friends"? Sabrina was her best friend now? How could I compete with this new Sabrina girl?

I thought and thought and tried to push down all the icky feelings that were coming up. What I wanted to do was cry, but that wouldn't help. I asked myself some questions:

Was I ready to give up Molly as a best friend?

The answer was a huge NO.

So what did I need to do to compete with Sabrina? Mr. Miller said if I did well in the commercial, I'd be in others. So that meant . . . I only had to land the full, and I'd be able to keep my BFF.

The thought made me feel shaky. However, I had some time to practice and land that full. Maybe even months!

I ran downstairs to check with my mom and dad. "Hey!" I yelled through the living room. "Do we know when I'm going to be in that commercial?" I asked. I was hoping they'd say, "Next year!"

Instead my dad said, "Oh, yeah. We just figured that out, actually. In two weeks they'll be shooting."

Two weeks?

Two weeks.

A huge knot twisted up my insides.

I stood still for a long time. Finally, a gush of I-gotta-do-something-right-now rushed through me. "MOM!" I yelled. "Can we go to the gym so I can practice?"

Her eyebrows scrunched together. "Tonight?" she asked.

I squared my shoulders. "Every night this week. The weekend too."

Mom and Dad shared a look. "I guess . . ." she said.

"Good," I said, the knot in my stomach loosening just a little. I ran up to my room and opened an email to Molly.

Dear Molly,

Your friend sounds so cool. I can't talk much, though — the shoot is in two weeks. I have to practice. I hope you have fun in your acting class. And I hope you have fun with Sabrina!

XOXO,

Olive

I closed my computer down but felt a little bad. I hadn't written "best friends forever" to close the email. But neither had Molly.

The twist on my insides was back. If only my insides twisting meant I could twist on the outside too.

Chapter 4

Molly Makes a Plan

Molly

UGH. Olive was so busy that she could barely even write to me. All because she was practicing her acting. *I* was supposed to be the actor in our friendship!

I started an email to her about three times. It started with:

Dear Olive,

Then the cursor stopped and blinked at me.

So, I opened up Skype to see if we could IM. Of course she wasn't there — she was too busy.

If Olive was already too busy for me, what if she got really, really famous? She would forget all about me.

Just as I was about to get off of Skype, I heard a noise that meant someone asked to be my friend. I checked. It was Sabrina!

I clicked on my new friend request. Then I pinged Sabrina with an IM. I got a little nervous — what if I said something stupid?

I swallowed and sat up straight. *Hi,* I wrote.

She wrote back, *Hi.*

Then nothing happened. So I wrote, *My best friend is in a commercial in Iowa. I'm a little jealous.*

Sabrina didn't say anything at first. Then she wrote, *Iowa? That is a dumb place for a commercial.*

I didn't know what to think about that. Iowa seemed pretty cool to me. And that seemed like a mean thing to say, especially about a place where Olive lived. I finally decided to write, *Olive says it's a pretty cool place.*

Sabrina wrote back, *Whatever. New York is normally where all the commercials are shot.*

I huffed out and wrote, *It seems like everyone is in a commercial but me!*

Nothing happened on the screen. I squirmed in my chair. Maybe I did say something stupid. But finally, Sabrina said, *Do you want to try to get in one? I bet there are some being shot in Central Park. Want to meet me there?*

SABRINA WAS GOING TO GET ME IN A COMMERCIAL!!

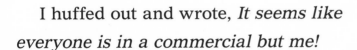

I settled down to write her and to seem a little cooler about the whole thing than I really felt. Sabrina didn't seem to be someone who liked really bouncy people. I never had to do that with Olive — she liked me just the way I was. But sometimes with new friends, you had to be different.

Sure, whatever, I wrote. *When should we meet?*

Sabrina wrote back, *Tomorrow around 4:00 by the Bethesda Fountain in Central Park. Can your mom take you there?*

I thought about it — Mom usually worked from home on those days. Without even asking her, I said, *YES. See you there!*

Sabrina pinged off, and I got up off my chair and jumped up and down a million times.

Finally. FINALLY. I would be in a commercial.
And Olive would think we were exactly the
same. This would all work out perfectly.

yipeeeeee

Except . . . I had to go tell my mom. That part
wasn't going to be easy. I squared my shoulders
and put on my nicest smile. "MOM!" I yelled.

Olive Flips for Her Friends

Olive

"OOF," I said as I fell on the mat for the 600th time. This time though, the wind was knocked right out of me.

I hadn't even done a half full. I could barely even get to the second handspring. Something felt really strange about the moves. But I was too frustrated to think it through.

Luckily, a few days ago, I'd decided to bring in reinforcements from my gymnastics team. I'd asked the best person on my team, plus a couple of others, to come help me. I was a little early, so I'd already been practicing. Not that it helped much.

"Hey, Olive!" I heard Maddie call out. She was the one on the team who could do anything, it seemed.

Two more of my teammates walked in too. Colette and Taylor. They were also really good. Plus, they were just pretty fun to hang around. Not as fun as Molly was, but still pretty fun.

"So what's this emergency?" Maddie asked as she set down her bag. She began stretching.

I bounced back and forth on my feet. "Wellll . . . ," I laughed and said all in one breath, "I'm going to be in a commercial and I'm supposed to do two back handsprings and a full and I can't do it and I'm afraid I'm going to get fired and then . . ." I didn't add that I was afraid Molly wouldn't want to be my friend anymore.

Maddie stopped stretching and just stared. So did Taylor and Colette. I wasn't sure what they were staring at exactly. Finally, Maddie spoke.

"But that's . . . ," she said.

Taylor said, "The commercial thing is super cool! Congratulations! But . . ."

And then Colette added, "Yeah, that's great. But that combination is . . . it's just . . ."

Maddie finished, "CRAZY HARD. Like, girls much older than us would have a hard time doing that!"

"Let's all try it once. We'll warm up a little," Maddie said.

After just a little bit, the girls were warmed up, and we took turns practicing it like 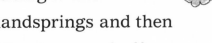 Mr. Miller said: two back handsprings and then a full. But it didn't work without a round-off.

Maddie went first. She sprinted down the mat, paused, turned around, and then did one back handspring, then barely made it to another back handspring. It looked awkward. It DEFINITELY needed a round-off. But Mr. Miller had asked me specifically about those moves.

So again and again, we all tried, and again and again, no one made it. None of us could get to the full twist!

By the end of an hour, I was drenched in sweat, and my legs were achy and shaky. We all looked at each other, and I knew it: It was time to call it a day.

We grabbed our bags, and Maddie put her hand on my shoulder. "I just don't think it's doable, not with us anyway. I think what he's asking for is too hard for our age. Maybe for any age?"

I smiled at them, but I couldn't help feeling sad all over. I couldn't tell Mr. Miller that I couldn't do it. If I did  that, he'd fire me. He'd never put me in another commercial again. And my best friend forever would be my best friend never.

"Thanks so much for coming, you guys. It was really fun to see you outside of the season anyway," I said.

They walked out the door, and I was left to think about how much I would miss Molly when she was gone.

Molly Makes It Happen

When we got to the fountain at Central Park, I looked all over for Sabrina. I saw her and her dad on a bench, so I dragged Mom over there.

Sabrina's dad had the same eyes as hers, but he had white skin and blonde hair instead of her black hair and brown skin. My mom smiled and put out her hand, "Hi, I'm Evelyn," she said to Sabrina's dad. He put out his hand and shook my mom's. "Pleasure to meet you. I'm Dan," he said.

Weirdly, they kept looking at each other. And my mom had a super silly smile on her face.

"Um, MOM," I said, trying to snap her out of it. It worked. She broke eye contact and said, "Yes, daughter of mine?"

"Can Sabrina and me walk around the fountain?" I asked.

"Sabrina and I," she said.

I made a joke my grandma always made, "Why would you and Sabrina want to go?" Only my mom and I cracked up, though Dan smiled a little. My mom said, "If it's okay with Dan, I'm fine with it."

Dan said, "Of course. We can sit and chat." He smiled a really big smile at my mom.

She smiled back, and it was like they forgot all about us. But I was fine with that. While my mom and Dan sat and talked, Sabrina and I could go anywhere we wanted! It was kind of perfect. I grabbed Sabrina's arm, and we walked away.

"Okay, where is this commercial being shot?" I asked.

Sabrina blinked. "What commercial?"

Then I blinked. "THE commercial!" was all I could think to say.

Sabrina stared.

I stared.

Finally I said, "Didn't you say you knew a commercial you could get me in?"

Sabrina scrunched her eyebrows down. "No. I said commercials are shot here a lot."

I thought back to our conversation. I guess that's what she said . . . only, she made it sound different. Like she could for sure get me in a commercial. I wondered if she did that on purpose. That made me feel really itchy.

We kept walking, but I wasn't sure what I should say to her. Suddenly it felt like I might have misheard everything. When I was about to tell her that we should go back to our parents, I saw him.

Bailey Scott.

Bailey Scott, the star of about 20 Nickelodeon shows. Bailey Scott, the ONLY boy I thought worthy of being crushed on.

Right there in
the park. And
there were cameras
everywhere.

I stopped and
gasped. "Look!" I
whispered to Sabrina.

Sabrina's eyes lit up. "OH MY GOSH!" she
said really loud.

"Shhhhhh!" I shhhhh'd.

In the whisperiest whisper I could
do, I said, "I think I see a trailer over there.
I bet if we introduce ourselves to him, he'd
definitely let us be in a show with him! Not
just a commercial!"

Sabrina's eyes got wide, and she nodded. We both tiptoed closer and closer and closer to the trailer. Before we got there, though, there was a barrier of some sort and some people standing around.

I saw an opening. When the person by the barrier was looking the other way, Sabrina and I snuck through. Then we ran around to the back of the trailer and hid.

NO ENTRY

By this time, I had a case of the giggles so bad, I wanted to explode. All of this was just so funny! Just a few minutes ago, we'd been at a fountain, talking about how MAYBE someone was shooting a commercial. And here we were on the set of . . . something, anyway. It all seemed too good to be true.

I couldn't help it; my giggles spilled over. Sabrina didn't giggle though, she just looked at me like she was annoyed. Just when I was going to tell Sabrina that she should lighten up a little, a voice called out, "Okay, girls, the show's over. Nothing funny here anymore."

I stopped laughing and gulped.

Chapter 7

Olive Mostly, Sort of, Almost Comes Clean

Olive

After practice, my mom sat in our truck waiting for me. I couldn't help feeling down.

"Uh-oh. Should we get some ice cream?" Mom asked. I shrugged, and her eyes got wide. "No comment? No opinion? We need ice cream STAT!" she practically yelled.

I smiled a little. Just a little.

"Do you want to talk about it?" she asked as she began driving.

I shook my head. All I could think about was how much fun Molly must be having with Sabrina. About how they'd talk about acting all the time, and then Molly would feel like she couldn't talk to me about anything. How I'd just be a boring girl from Iowa with only farm animals to talk about. Even though Molly loved hearing about my farm, how long would that last if she had a shiny new acting friend?

Mom pulled up to an ice-cream store. We were in Sioux City for practice, so I wasn't sure where we were. Except, when I looked out the window, I saw the mattress store!

I looked at Mom with wide eyes. "Wha . . .?"

"I think you're pretty nervous about this commercial, honey. I think you need to talk to Mr. Miller. Or at least see the store you'll be advertising. What do you think about looking at some mattresses and then grabbing some ice cream?" My mom is funny sometimes. She'll ask something like it's a question. But really she was TELLING me I'd be going inside to look around.

When I walked in, the floor had a ton of beds lined up on display. They all looked soft.

"There's my little superstar!" Mr. Miller's voice boomed. He walked over to me and my mom. He smiled at Mom and put his hand out for me to high-five him. So I high-fived him. Grown-ups are weird like that.

My mom said, "I'm going to check out some mattresses," and walked away. Even though I knew she didn't need a new mattress.

"So are you just here to check out the store?" Mr. Miller asked.

I swallowed. I gathered my courage. And I said . . .

Nothing. I couldn't seem to say anything!

I just nodded. I had flashes of Molly and Sabrina in my head, and I couldn't bring myself to give up on my best friend yet. I still had to try for the commercial.

"Well, come check out this mattress!" He took me over to a place in a corner where there was only one bed. "This is the 'jumping' mattress," he said. "Some kids like to jump on beds, so I have one just for them. Want to try?"

That actually did sound fun. So I nodded again and climbed on. I jumped and jumped and jumped! Higher and higher. Until finally,

I was able to do a
backflip and land on
my feet on the bed.
Pretty soon I was
giggling, and my mom
was there too, watching.

Mr. Miller beamed.
"I'm so lucky I ran into
you at the feed store. To be able to find the
perfect gymnast for my 'Spring into Savings'
sale . . . I tell you, I'm a lucky guy. It looks like
your daughter can do anything."

I stopped jumping and climbed off the bed.
The full kept popping into my head. I couldn't
do EVERYTHING, that was for sure.

The other thing I couldn't do? Tell Mr. Miller
the truth.

Chapter 8

Molly Comes Clean

Molly

Sabrina's eyes were wide. I could feel my eyes were really wide too. My body felt loose like I was made of spaghetti.

We were in SO MUCH TROUBLE.

"Um," I said, "we got lost. Do you know where the hot dog truck is?"

Sabrina gave me a weird look. I shrugged. Maybe they'd believe we thought the trailer was a hot dog truck!

"You need to move on out of here. Bailey Scott isn't even shooting today," said the woman. She was dressed in a T-shirt that read "GYMNAST PARADISE CREW." That must have been the show they were working on, and it must have been brand new. That was super exciting, except it made me miss Olive even more. She would have loved a show like that.

The woman grabbed our arms and walked us around the trailer. We were going the opposite way we snuck in, which was pretty cool because we got to see more of the set.

There were gymnasts flipping here and there and warming up. I thought that Olive might be perfect for this show. After her commercial, she should try out for this.

I watched as a kid around 12 years old did a whole bunch of complicated springing and jumping. And then I had an idea.

I twisted around to face the woman. "This is a gymnastics show, right?" I said. The woman nodded but kept walking. "Well, I know the best gymnast kid the world has ever seen!" My voice got louder and louder.

The woman tightened her grip and said, "Shhh. Keep your voice down!"

Telling me to be quiet was a big mistake on her part. Now I knew how to get some attention. "Hey, everyone!" I yelled. "I KNOW THE BEST GYMNAST EVER, AND SHE SHOULD BE ON THIS SHOW!"

"What is this racket?" a voice called out. Another woman came charging over. When she turned sideways, I could see the word "DIRECTOR" on her back.

I gasped. This was it! "Excuse-me-ma'am-but-I-know-someone-who-should-be-in-this-show!" I said, the words all tangled. She frowned.

"I'm so sorry, Abby," the woman holding us said. "I couldn't keep her quiet."

Abby looked at me and said, "That's okay. I was a kid just like her once." She smiled, and I smiled back.

"My best friend is a gymnast!" I said. Then before anyone could shush me, I went on, "And she should totally be in this show!"

Abby looked at Sabrina and said, "You know, there's no room in this show, but I am shooting a commercial that she might be perfect for."

I stopped dead still. What was happening?

Sabrina's eyes lit up. "I'd love to be in a commercial!"

"Wait . . ." I said. I hadn't meant Sabrina!

"Have you ever been in a commercial?" Abby asked.

Sabrina, her eyes wide, shook her head.

My mouth almost hit the floor. "Wait," I said, "you've never been in a commercial? I thought you've been in seven!"

Sabrina gave me a dirty look. "I was ALMOST in seven commercials. I never got the part." She turned to Abby. "I'd love to be in it."

I couldn't believe what was happening. All of this had backfired! Plus, my new friend had been lying to me this whole time! She wasn't my friend at all.

As if to prove it, Sabrina walked off with Abby, not even looking at me. The woman

holding me didn't have to keep going. I wriggled out of her grasp and ran.

I ran all the way back to the fountain where Dan and my mom were. They were laughing hard at something together. But nothing was funny right now.

"Where's Sabrina?" Dan asked.

It took all of my willpower not to cry. "They asked her to be in a commercial," I said. "Just follow that path. She's talking to the director."

I saw my mom's look. She knew how sad I was. She stood up and said, "I hope to keep in touch, Dan. I'm going to take Molly home."

We walked fast to the subway and got on the train. I kept my tears from falling, but the whole way home, I kept thinking about how

miserable I was. About how I'd acted different with Sabrina, but I didn't have to do that with Olive. Except . . . I had. I hadn't been honest with Olive. Now I only wanted to do one thing. When we got to our apartment, I sprinted to my room and opened an email.

Dear Olive,

I feel like I haven't been a good friend lately. I was so jealous of you that you got to be in a commercial! I'm seriously so excited for you!

And I really was! I loved it when good things happened for Olive.

I have had a really bad time, though. Someone I thought was my friend, wasn't.

I told Olive everything. I just hoped she could forgive me for being so selfish.

Olive Makes a Plan

I stared at Molly's email. How awful for her! And how dumb I'd been for thinking she was replacing me. It was my turn to come clean to her right away.

I told her the whole thing: how I'd tried and tried, but I just couldn't come up with a way to make the combination Mr. Miller wanted work. I sent off the email, and almost immediately, Molly wrote back. She wanted to IM, so I pulled up Skype, and she pinged on right away.

Ohmygosh, that sounds so awful!

It is! It sounds so awful that Sabrina got that commercial too. All because you were trying to help me! Thank you for that by the way.

I should have done it sooner. But you WOULD have been perfect for that show, Olive.

I wish you were here! Then maybe YOU could be in this commercial instead of me.

Molly, what am I going to do? I have to tell him, don't I?

. . .

64

 Molly!

 Sorry! I was thinking. I do have an idea. And it's not really about you telling him . . .

 ???

 Listen, he's a grown-up, right?

Yes . . .

Sometimes grown-ups don't know what they want.

So maybe just try a combination that works and don't say anything about it! Maybe he won't be able to tell.

I thought about that. It was true — the combination Mr. Miller wanted me to do didn't make much sense. And it wasn't just me who thought that! The other girls on my team and I all tried it. If I tried something different without saying anything, it just might work.

 I wish you were here.

Yeah, that would be cool.

 I wish I could get you in a commercial. For real. Not the way Sabrina did it.

LOL You mean the way she lied about everything? Yeah . . . You know, no one could ever compare to you, right? We are best friends forever. No matter what!

That line definitely made me teary.

 Same over here. You are always my best friend.

 Good luck, Olive! Let me know how it goes.

 xoxoxoxoxoxoxoxoxoxoxoxo <3 <3 <3 <3

I shut down Skype and felt a million times better. All I needed was a little pep talk from my best friend.

I just wished I could help her the way she'd helped me.

Molly Mopes but Then Un-Mopes

Molly

Everything felt better. Everything! Olive and I were A-okay. Nothing was going to stop our friendship. I felt almost perfect except . . .

Not quite. I couldn't help it. I just felt down.

I moped my way to the kitchen and crumpled into a seat by the dining room table. I put my head in my hands and sighed.

"Molly, is there something wrong?" my mom finally asked.

"I'm going to quit acting class, I think," I said, not looking at her.

She put her papers aside and faced me. "What's going on, honey?"

I held in my tears as best I could. But maybe one or two squeezed out. "I am just not very good, clearly. Sabrina got that commercial and didn't do anything! And I'm really happy for Olive but —"

"But, you are sad for yourself," she finished. I nodded. She took a deep breath.

"If people quit every time they got stuck, do you know how much would get done?" she asked. I shrugged. "Nothing," she said. Then she leaned in and put her finger under my chin. "You, Molly Riley Walker, are no quitter. You come from a long line of proud women. Proud, ingenious, brilliant, determined women. Women who were given nothing and had the whole world against them. And they worked hard to make lives for themselves, no matter what."

I swallowed. I knew things were important when Mom brought in all my grandmas.

"Okay," I said, squaring my shoulders. "I'm not going to quit. I'm going to be determined."

My mom laughed and hugged me. "You have never been anything but. You never know what opportunities will come your way!"

Chapter 11

Olive Springs into Savings

Olive

I could barely breathe. There were cameras everywhere and so many lights! They'd even given me my own chair. And someone was putting makeup on me.

My mom and dad stood in a corner. When I looked at them, they both waved excitedly. All I could do was gulp.

The director came over to me and said, "Okay, Olive, are you ready?" I nodded. "Here's how it's going to go," he said. "Mr. Miller is going to say these lines: 'Here at Miller

Mattress Emporium, we are flipping for these prices! Come on down and SPRING into savings!'" I nodded. The director went on, "So after he says the word 'SPRING,' you do your thing, okay?"

Suddenly, I lost all my nerve. Who was I to change anything? My hands felt sweaty and my throat felt dry. But the director had left already, not even waiting for my answer.

"Let's try a run or two before we start filming!" the director called. He sat in a chair and said, "Places."

I went to where I was supposed to stand. I took a deep breath and thought of Molly — sometimes grown-ups didn't know everything. And I knew gymnastics! My courage came back, and I could feel my hands tingling. I really thought I could do it!

"Okay, let's go!" the director said.

Mr. Miller said, "Here at Miller Mattress Enforium . . . ," then he started laughing. The director did too. I did not.

"Sorry! Sorry!" Mr. Miller said. "Let's try that again."

I took a deep breath and thought about my moves: a round-off to a back handspring to a full. My whole body was ready.

The director said, "Okay, and go."

"Here at Miller Mattress Emporium," said Mr. Miller in a huge voice, "we are flipping for these prices! Come on down and SPRING —"

I heard the word "spring," and I was off. I sprinted a few steps, did the round-off, right into the back handspring, and then threw myself in the air . . .

AND DID THE FULL!

I couldn't believe it! Everyone clapped.

Mr. Miller came up to me and patted my shoulder. "Ms. Olive, I have a cousin in New York who owns a mattress store out there. He and I try to outdo each other with commercials. I feel kind of bad for him right now! His star quit on him just yesterday. Now he has no one to do his commercial while I have the best gymnast in all the Midwest!"

I blushed. That was definitely not true.

"You liked the combination?" I croaked.

"It was perfect!" he said. "I can't even remember what I asked you to do, so whatever this was, it was perfect."

I beamed. Everything felt right as rain at that moment. I felt like I could do the commercial a million times. If only Molly could do a commercial too.

Then it hit me!

I tapped Mr. Miller on the shoulder. "Did you say your cousin needs an actor in New York?"

Mr. Miller said, "Yes! My cousin Ernest. Why?"

"I know the perfect actor for the commercial. And I know a perfect way to make both your commercials great!"

Molly's Big Break

Molly

Our landline was ringing. It was so annoying. "GET THE PHONE, DAMIEN!" I yelled. I don't even know why we keep a landline. No one has those anymore.

Damien yelled back, "NO! I'M PLAYING VIDEO GAMES!"

Brothers are the worst. I closed down the email that I was writing to Olive. I hadn't heard anything about the commercial, and I was dying! I had so many questions: Did she do the new combination? Did it work? Did anyone say anything? Did she land the full twist?

I got the phone. "Hello." I said as snotty as I could.

"Hello, I'm wondering if I can speak to Molly Walker or her mother," a male voice on the other end said.

"MOM!" I yelled. She should have gotten it anyway. But she was probably working like she always did. She loved doing spreadsheets, it seemed.

I heard my mom pick up the phone and went back to my email. Then I thought — wait. They wanted to talk to ME too. So I went to where my mom was with the phone. I could only hear her half of the conversation.

"Uh-huh," she said. "Yes . . . Okay . . . I think she'd love to! . . . . Okay, let me ask her, and I'll get back to you."

By this time, I was literally trying to stick my ear on the phone. She pushed me away gently and hung up.

"What would I love to do?" I asked.

"Who said that was about you?" my mom said.

"The guy asked for you or me," I said, rolling my eyes.

My mom chuckled. "Well, you were right. I think you're going to like this a lot. You ready?"

"YES!" I said, bouncing up and down. I already felt excited, and I didn't know why. My mom had a twinkle in her eye that she normally didn't have.

Finally, she said, "That was Ernest Miller. He wants to know if you want to be in his commercial! You just have to try out to see if you're a good fit."

My eyes got so big, it felt like they turned into planets. My whole body felt like electricity was zinging through it. I could barely make out any of my own thoughts — it was as if I short-circuited like a robot!

"Molly?" my mom asked.

"YEEEESSSSSS!" I yelled. "YES YES YES YES!!! YES I WANT TO BE IN IT!" I zoomed around the room. I caught a glimpse of Damien, who had come from the hallway. Probably because I was yelling and zooming.

My mom laughed and laughed. "Okay, okay, we get it," she said. "Stand still so I can tell you about it. Because it gets better."

Now *that* I didn't believe. How could it get any BETTER?

My mom slowed me down, and I stopped. She said, "Ernest Miller is Matthew Miller's brother. Matthew Miller owns a mattress shop in Sioux City, Iowa, and that's where Olive is in the commercial. So Olive heard that Ernest had some bad luck with an actor, and she had an idea. She thought they could cast you! But here's the best part — it will actually be one commercial. Since the mattress stores are part of the same family-owned chain, they'll save money by doing just one commercial. And you and Olive will be in it together!"

I almost fainted with happiness. What was better than being in a commercial? Being in it with your best friend. Even if you lived millions of miles away.

Chapter 13

Olive and Molly Together

Olive

I had my mom's laptop open, and Molly was ready on Skype. We had both been sent videos of our commercial, and we sat down — all of us — to watch it.

Molly moved her computer so the camera showed all around her place. Her mom waved to us, and her little brother, Damien, stuck out his tongue. We got to use Skype with ACTUAL phone and face time, since this was a special occasion. We had decided to do that only a couple times a year to stay pen pal best friends. But sometimes, you just had to talk.

"Okay," Molly's mom said, "let's start the DVD on the count of three so we can watch it at the same time."

I felt nervous for some reason. Molly and I shared a look and then started giggling. I could tell she felt nervous too. But our looks to each other said, "It's going to be great!"

I whispered to her, "I can't wait to see you in it!"

She grinned and said, "I can't wait to see you, either!"

"One . . . two . . . ," Molly's mom counted down.

All of us shouted, "THREE!" and turned on the commercial.

It started with Matthew Miller. "Here at Miller Mattress Emporium in Sioux City, Iowa, we are flipping for these prices! Come on down and SPRING —"

Then the camera zoomed in on me. I could feel my cheeks get red. The camera showed me doing the round-off, the back handspring, and a full twist in the air.

"HOLY WOW!" Molly said. "Olive, you're amazing!"

I smiled, but then I made my eyes wide. "Shh! You're next!"

Then the camera cut to Ernest Miller. "Springing into savings? We've got savings too! Here in New York City, we're JUMPING FOR JOY!"

The camera zoomed in on Molly, jumping like a maniac on one of the mattresses. She jumped down and stood by Ernest. "Mr. Miller," she said, "your mattresses are the best for jumping. I bet they're pretty good for sleeping on too."

I gasped. Molly seemed like a natural-born actor. She said the line perfectly and even gave a wink after. "MOLLY!" I yelled. "You are so good at that!"

The screen split, and one side was Matthew and me, and the other was Molly and Ernest. The best thing though? Molly and I were shoulder to shoulder, like we were actually together in the same place.

All of us on the commercial moved our arms in a "come here" motion and said at the same time, "COME ON DOWN TO MILLER MATTRESS EMPORIUM FOR YOUR FLIPPING, SPRINGING, JUMPING SAVINGS!"

We all clapped. That was probably the best commercial I'd ever seen. Especially because it showed Molly and me together.

After everyone left, Molly and I sat on Skype.

"I knew you were good at gymnastics, Olive," Molly said, "But I didn't know you were that good! It's like you're in the Olympics or something!"

I blushed. "I couldn't have done it without your idea! If I'd tried to stick to Mr. Miller's idea, I could have never done it."

"That's because the combination was wrong," Molly said, "not because of you. You are amazing. And anyway, I only got the commercial because of you."

I shook my head hard. She was totally wrong. "No way! I suggested you for sure. But they all made it clear to me that you had to try out. Because they wanted you to do some acting, and if you couldn't do it, well . . . they would have picked someone else. Mr. Miller said you blew his brother away!"

Molly smiled and ducked her head. "He did say he wanted me for more commercials."

I smiled HUGE. This made me happier than anything else could have.

"I guess we both have some pretty great talent, huh?" Molly said.

I nodded. "And lots of work to do."

She echoed, "And lots of work to do."

"At least through all this work, we'll have each other, right?" Molly said.

We said at the same exact time, because that's what best friends do:

"BEST FRIENDS FOREVER."

About the Author

Megan Atwood lives and works in Minneapolis, Minnesota. She has written more than 35 children's books and teaches creative writing at Hamline University. When she is not writing books or teaching, she is inflicting love and affection on her cats and dreaming up more characters to keep her company. She also is trying to find more time to write personal letters to her loved ones, much like Molly and Olive.

Megan Atwood

About the Illustrator

Originally from London, Gareth now lives in beautiful Somerset with his wife and two boys. He works from his home studio alongside his ever-faithful assistant, Herbie the Jack Russell. After studying illustration at Bournemouth College of Art and Design and working in-house for the majority of his career, Gareth took the plunge to go freelance seven years ago and hasn't looked back.

Gareth Llewhellin

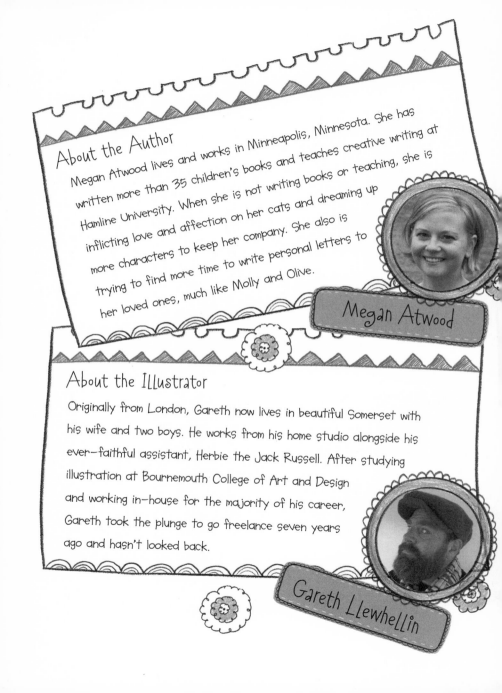

Glossary

back handspring—a kind of backflip

barrier—a bar, fence, or other object that prevents people from entering an area

emporium—a store selling a lot of items

exchange—to trade one thing for another

feed—food for animals

full—a gymnastics move in which the gymnast spins in a complete circle in the air

honest—truthful

jealous—wanting something that someone else has

recognize—to know something from seeing it before

round-off—a gymnastics move that involves jumping from feet to hands and back with a half turn

seriously—not lightly

Talk It Out

1. Was Olive right to worry about her friendship with Molly? Why or why not?.

2. Molly changes her personality around Sabrina. Do you think she's right to do so? Explain your answer.

3. Explain why Olive didn't tell Mr. Miller the truth. Describe a time when you didn't think you could tell the truth.

Write It Out

1. Write a description of Sabrina's character. What is her personality like?

2. Pretend you are either Molly or Olive. Write an apology to your best friend for not being completely honest. What would you say to make her forgive you?

3. Have you ever changed your personality or the way you act around someone else? Describe the experience.

A Letter for You!

Hi, Everyone!

It's Olive here. I was so NERVOUS when I decided to be in that commercial. But Molly had some great ideas from her acting class about how I could get more comfortable. Want to try? This game is called "Mirror."

First, get your best friend to help you. She can be right beside you or she can be on some sort of video chat, like Molly and I do!

Second, stand in front of each other. One of you should start moving really slowly, and the other person has to follow along and mimic the same movements. If you're like Molly and me, you'll start giggling right away. But that's okay! Just try to keep eye contact the whole time.

Molly says this helps you pay attention to people around you — actors have to respond to anyone else they're acting with. And you get to pretend to be your best friend! That part is my favorite.

Thanks for reading this! I hope you have fun playing Mirror!

All love,

Olive

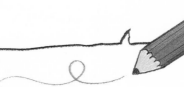

The fun doesn't stop here!

Discover more at www.capstonekids.com

Videos & Contests

Games & Puzzles

Friends & Favorites

Authors & Illustrators

Find cool websites and more books like this one at
www.facthound.com. Just type in the
Book ID: 9781515829225 and you're ready to go!